arc • anthill B basket • butterfly

2-5

bouncing • buttercups bird's nest • bush •

C calico coat • camping • cattails • castle •

crow • cooking cricket • crest D dog tag •

door dragonfly • dandelions • dove

floor lamp • freckles fern • flowers

G glasses • gerbil • gold • grapes Gary •

hair spray hair dryer • hairbrush • haircut •

• ice fishing icicles • ice cube J jars •

juggling • jester jelly beans •

• karate • kilts kicking • kickstands

• leather jacket • lake • light lemons •

lovebirds M makeup • mama • motorbike •

mail • mailbox • mountains • mouse

Every letter of the alphabet is hidden in the pictures of this book. So are many things that start with each letter. (There are things that end with the sound of X, too!) How many can you find? Look at the beginning and end of the book for help!

Peanut Butter and Jellyfishes

A Very Silly Alphabet Book

by Brian P. Cleary

illustrations by Betsy E. Snyder

M Millbrook Press · Minneapolis

A is for antelopes forming an arc.

B begins birch trees
with bubblegum bark.

C is for cat
with a calico coat

who camps
by a castle
and cooks
by a moat.

D starts dalmatian, a dog who's been spotted.

E is for each evergreen Elvis potted.

F starts flamingo

and **G** begins Gary, the gerbil

that **H** helps us say
is quite **h**airy.

I is for ice cream,
the size of an igloo.

J is for jars full of jasmine and wig glue.

K starts karate
and kangaroos kissing,
and kilt-wearing kittens
whose kickstands
are missing.

L is for letters
that start the word llama.

M

begins motorbike, makeup, and mama.

N is for newt
with a necklace
of noodles.

O begins ostrich
with oats
by the oodles.

P is for patterns
on plates and on dishes,

and plain peanut butter
on pink jellyfishes.

Q starts a quail
who is quiet
and quivers.

R
is for rafting
red raspberry rivers.

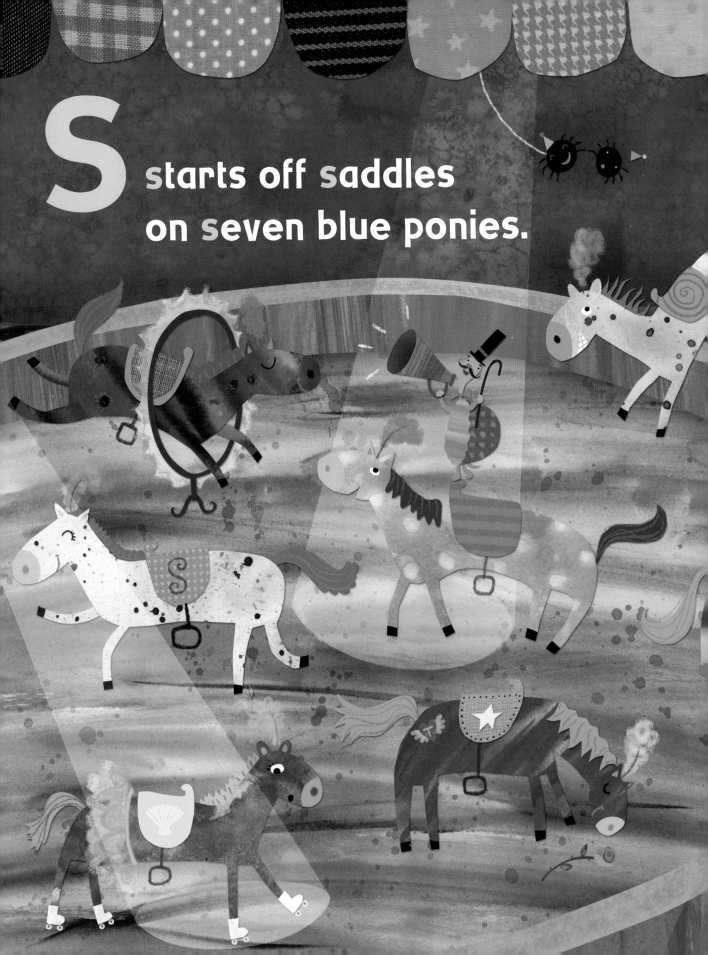

S starts off saddles on seven blue ponies.

T is for tents
filled with
Tinas
and Tonys.

University of U

U Café

U starts umbrellas
unfolding uptown
and underpants
on an unusual clown.

V starts a **v**eil-wearing **v**olleyball player.

W starts Will,
who's a wallaby weigher.

X is the end sound in o**x** and in a**x**e.

Y starts Yolanda
with six yellow yaks.

Z begins zebra and zipper and zoo.

I know my ABCs—
how about you?

To Connor —BPC

To Gram and Mom, for always believing in the Invisible Lady with One Orange Leg —BES

Millbrook Press, Inc.
A division of Lerner Publishing Group
241 First Avenue North
Minneapolis, MN 55401 U.S.A.

Website address: www.lernerbooks.com

Library of Congress Cataloging-in-Publication Data

Cleary, Brian P., 1959–
    Peanut butter and jellyfishes : a very silly alphabet book / by Brian P. Cleary ; illustrations by Betsy E. Snyder.
        p.   cm.
      ISBN-13: 978-0-8225-6188-0 (lib. bdg. : alk. paper)
      ISBN-10: 0-8225-6188-3 (lib. bdg. : alk. paper)
      1. English language—Alphabet—Juvenile poetry. 2. Children's poetry, American. 3. Alphabet rhymes. I. Snyder, Betsy E., ill. II. Title.
    PS3553.L39144P43 2007
    428.1'3—dc22   2006012057

Manufactured in the United States of America
1 2 3 4 5 6 – DP – 12 11 10 09 08 07

N noodles • necklace • nest  newt • night •

note • nightcap O ostrich • oodles • owl

P pretzels • pansies party hats • pitcher •

peppermints purse • puffer fish plates

pasta • pink lemonade • pepperoni pizza

R river • ruby • rabbits rainbow trout • raven

S squirrel • spiderweb • shouting • snail

stirrups saddles • star • stitching • skates •

turtle • tattoo • top hat tricks • tutu • tents •

underpants • university umbrellas

veil • volcano V-neck • vest W Will

water • wedding ring • whale wedding

xylophone Y Yolanda • yarn

Z zoo • Zachary zigzag